A MYSTERIOUS LEGEND . . .

A curtain parted and an elderly woman whose face was so wrinkled it was hard to see her eyes shuffled into the room. "Sit down, *niños*. My great-grandson tells me that you are needy. I will give you a reading."

Katie frowned. "I don't think you understand, ma'am. Pepe told us to come here because we need information about our dad. We really don't have time for anything else."

"Sit," the old woman commanded. She closed her eyes and began swaying back and forth. In moments a strange, high-pitched wail came from her lips. Then she stopped. Her eyes opened and she stared straight at Katie. She pointed a long, bony finger in Katie's face. "You . . . you have the key. But you must be very careful. I have seen danger. Your friends may be your enemies. And your enemies will come for you. I see that you are part of the legend."

CURSE
OF THE RUINS

A YEARLING BOOK

Published by
Bantam Doubleday Dell Books for Young Readers
a division of
Bantam Doubleday Dell Publishing Group, Inc.
1540 Broadway
New York, New York 10036

The trademarks Yearling® and Dell® are registered in the U.S. Patent and Trademark Office and in other countries.
Visit us on the Web!
www.bdd.com

Educators and librarians, visit the
BDD Teacher's Resource Center at
www.bdd.com/teachers

ISBN: 0-440-41225-0

Series design: Barbara Berger

Interior illustration by Michael David Biegel

Printed in the United States of America

March 1998

10 9 8 7 6 5 4 3

Dear Readers:

Real adventure is many things—it's danger and daring and sometimes even a struggle for life or death. From competing in the Iditarod dogsled race across Alaska to sailing the Pacific Ocean, I've experienced some of this adventure myself. I try to capture this spirit in my stories, and each time I sit down to write, that challenge is a bit of an adventure in itself.

You're all a part of this adventure as well. Over the years I've had the privilege of talking with many of you in schools, and this book is the result of hearing firsthand what you want to read about most—power-packed adventure and excitement.

You asked for it—so hang on tight while we jump into another thrilling story in my World of Adventure.

Gary Paulsen

CURSE OF THE RUINS

CHAPTER 1

"We've landed, Katie. You can open your eyes now."

"Very funny." Thirteen-year-old Katherine Crockett gave her brother a look of disgust, flipped her long, sandy blond hair behind her shoulder, and stood to retrieve her overnight bag from the compartment above her head.

"Sam, you really shouldn't give Katie a hard time about flying." A tall African American boy across the aisle folded his arms. "Your dad wouldn't like it. And besides," he said with a snort, "some people can't help it if they're total wimps and have to use the barf bag before the plane even gets off the ground."

Katie glared at the tall boy. "Shala, if you think that being my cousin will keep me from hurting you—think again." She lifted her chin and stepped into the aisle.

"She's right, Shala. Being her cousin won't save you. I'm her brother, older brother to be exact, and it hasn't helped me a bit."

"I heard that." Katie was nearly at the front of the small plane. She turned and made a face. "Let's not get too carried away, *o ancient one.* You're only ten minutes older, and our birth certificates say we're twins, so that makes us equal enough in the age department."

Sam had opened his mouth to set her straight when a duffel bag came flying across the aisle and hit him in the chest.

"Here." Shala chuckled. "If you're smart you'll call it even and catch up with her before she gets to your dad first and our vacation in New Mexico starts off on the wrong foot."

"You have a point there." Sam edged around a woman in front of him and yelled over the heads of the other passengers. "Wait up, Katie. Dad said we should stay together, remember? San Marcos is right on the Mexican border. A town like this could be a rough place . . . for a little girl."

But Katie was already off the plane and heading for the terminal. She hurried through the glass doors and scanned the faces of the people in the waiting area, hoping to see her father's familiar salt-and-pepper beard.

"Excuse me, miss." A thin man with bushy black eyebrows and a thick Spanish accent stepped in front of her. "You look as if you need assistance. Perhaps I could hold your belongings while you try to locate your party."

"No . . . thank you." Katie moved a few steps away and glanced behind her to see if the boys were coming. Suddenly the man yanked her overnight bag from her fingers and darted through the crowd.

"Hey!" Katie yelled, charging after him. "Somebody stop that man!"

"Katie's in trouble!" Sam shouted. "Come on, Shala."

The two boys pushed past the new arrivals

3

and ran into the small airport lobby. They could see the top of Katie's head bobbing up and down as she blasted through the crowd in front of them.

Shala spotted something lying on the lobby floor. He scooped it up and sprinted after Sam.

Behind them an alarm went off. Airport security guards were blowing whistles and shouting in Spanish.

Katie saw the man she was after make a sudden turn at a bank of lockers. She chased him down a narrow corridor and started to follow him through a side exit.

Just as she shoved the unmarked door open, a hand with a grip like steel locked on to her arm. "Hold it right there, young lady."

Katie struggled and looked up into the face of a police officer. "That man—" She pointed at the thief, who had already stopped a taxi and was hastily climbing inside. "He stole my bag—and you're letting him get away."

Sam came crashing down the hallway with Shala close behind. "Are you all right, Katie? What happened?"

Katie blew air threw her teeth, still furious at the policeman. "I'm fine. But some guy ripped off my bag. I almost caught up with him when this bozo came along and let him get away."

Shala was breathing hard. "What . . . were you going to do with him . . . if you caught him?"

Katie rolled her eyes. "Ask him to the prom. What do you think I was going to do? Get my bag back, of course."

Five officers now surrounded them. The one still holding Katie's arm said something to the others in Spanish. Then he turned back to the three of them. "You will follow me. All of you are officially under arrest."

CHAPTER 2

"We told you." Sam wearily dropped to the wooden bench on the other side of the police sergeant's desk. "We were never in Mexico. Check with the airlines. We flew straight to New Mexico, we didn't cross the border, and we weren't trying to avoid customs. A thief stole my sister's bag and we were just trying to get it back."

"If you'll call the Hotel Monterrey and ask for my father, Professor William Crockett, he'll clear all this up in no time." Katie leaned on the desk. "He was supposed to meet us at the airport, but when your men arrested us we never got the chance to find him."

The sergeant nodded patiently. "You say your father is a professor of archaeology and that he is currently working in one of the ruins not far from the city?"

Shala, who was sitting on the bench beside Sam, let out a long breath. "That's what we told you. Let's see . . . is it eleven times so far? My uncle, their father, is expecting us to join him today so that he can take us out to the dig. You've searched us and our luggage. We're obviously not hiding anything. Why not let us go so we can get on with our vacation?"

A young police officer walked into the room and delivered a piece of paper. The sergeant read it quickly. He placed it on the desk in front of him and folded his hands. "It is true that we found nothing suspicious in your luggage and your papers seem to be in order. But there is one part of your story that does not seem to check out. There is no Professor Crockett registered at the Hotel Monterrey."

"What?" Sam jumped up. "Are you sure?

Maybe there's more than one Hotel Monterrey in San Marcos."

The sergeant shook his head. "I assure you there is only one. Now." He stood and walked around the desk. "The question is, what should be done with the three of you?"

"Well." Katie put her hands on her hips. "If you were real policemen, you would go get my bag back from that stupid crook and then help us find my dad."

Sam elbowed her. "Uh . . . what my sister means is that there is obviously some kind of weird mix-up going on here and we would really appreciate any help you could give us in locating our father."

"Of course. I have my officers inquiring as to his whereabouts even as we speak. We will also check with the federal officials about the ruins you mentioned. In the meantime, since we have no place to keep you other than a jail cell, I have decided to release the three of you—on one condition."

"Cool." Shala stood up. "What is it?"

"You will remember that you are in New Mexico now. And as guests of our state you will abide by our laws. If anyone other than a police officer should contact you about this incident you will report it to me at once. Is this understood?"

"Got it." Sam pushed the other two toward the door. "Can we get our stuff back now?"

The sergeant called to an officer and instructed him to take the three to the front desk and give them their belongings. "Enjoy your stay in San Marcos. And contrary to what you may think, I wish you much luck in locating your father." The sergeant followed them to the door. "Rest assured, we will be in touch."

CHAPTER 3

"Now what?" Sam set his suitcase on the cracked sidewalk outside the police station.

Katie reached for a small, sturdy chain she wore around her neck and pulled out a square leather purse attached to it. She unzipped the pouch, searched through her traveler's checks and identification papers, and found a worn envelope. "Here's Dad's last letter. Look, right here he says he'll meet us at the airport today and if there are any problems he'll be staying at the Hotel Monterrey, where he's booked rooms for all of us."

"There could be a problem." Shala pulled a wallet-sized photograph of Katie from his pocket. "I found this on the floor in the airport lobby. Did one of you drop it?"

Katie read the back. "That's my handwriting. I sent this to Dad right after school pictures came out. Why would it be in the airport?"

"There are a couple of possibilities." Shala's face was grim. "Either Uncle William was at the airport and accidentally dropped it. Or the man who stole your bag had it and was using the photo to identify you for some reason."

"But how could that creep have gotten my picture?" Katie's eyes widened. "Unless something happened to Dad."

"Calm down." Sam sat on his suitcase. "Don't go jumping to conclusions. The guy could have been a pickpocket. He probably swiped Dad's wallet earlier and read your letters. He took one look at your wimpy picture and decided to wait for you in the airport because you looked like an easy mark."

"I do not look like an easy mark." Katie

squared her shoulders. "And another thing—"

"We need some answers." Shala stepped to the curb. "I say we get a taxi and go to the hotel. Maybe Uncle William left a message with the desk."

"Pssst. *Gringos.* I have something for you."

They turned. The voice was coming from the alley. A small Mexican American boy peeked around the corner. He held up a teal-colored canvas bag.

"Hey! That's my overnight bag." Katie rushed to the corner. "Where'd you get it?"

The boy stepped back into the shadows and shrugged. "Pepe knows about everything that goes on in San Marcos. My cousin found this bag in the garbage. I knew it was yours. So I brought it to you." He held it out to her.

Katie grabbed it. "It's empty. And somebody has ripped out the lining."

The boy put his hands up. "I am innocent. I am merely returning your property—an act for which most wealthy tourists would reward me generously." He held out his hand.

"Thanks a lot." Katie scowled.

Shala took the bag. "Look at the way these cuts are made. Someone was careful to only slice the lining, not the bag itself. They must have thought something was hidden behind the lining and they were worried about damaging it." He looked at Pepe. "Do you know who did this?"

"Better question," Sam said, moving close to the boy. "*Why* did they do this?"

Pepe shook his head. "Not so fast. I have not survived this long on the streets of San Marcos by *giving* away information."

Sam reached into his jeans and took out a couple of dollars. "Here. Now, what's the story?"

Pepe took the money and stuffed it deep in his pocket. "The one who took your bag is not from San Marcos. He is an outsider, hired to meet you at the airport. And your *amigo* is right. The bag is torn like that because he was searching for something he believes you are carrying."

Katie frowned. "What in the world would I have that somebody would go to all this trouble to get?"

Pepe shrugged. "That I cannot tell you. But I would be very careful, *señorita.* If these men did not find the thing they were looking for in your bag, they will try again." He turned to walk back down the alley.

"Wait." Sam grabbed the boy's shoulder. "Can you tell us where the Hotel Monterrey is from here?"

Pepe's face brightened. "It is my business to offer assistance to poor lost tourists—for a small fee, of course."

"Of course." Sam gave him another dollar.

Pepe stepped into the street and pointed up the road. "Take Desert Avenue. Turn left at the square. The hotel is on Piedra Street. It's a good choice. Hot water and everything."

"One more question." Sam held a dollar over Pepe's palm. "What have you heard about an American archaeologist named William Crockett?"

Pepe snatched the money and shoved it in his pocket. "At this time I cannot say. But I will be very glad to ask around and bring this information to your hotel tonight."

Pepe hailed a taxi for them. "You will not be sorry that you have hired me, tourists. I know this town like the back of my hand. Anything you want"—he snapped his fingers—"Pepe will find a way to make it yours."

CHAPTER 4

"Yes, there was a Professor Crockett registered here." A swarthy man with a long nose stood behind the counter looking down at his logbook. "But he checked out several days ago."

"That's impossible." Katie tried to pry the book from the man's hands. "Didn't he reserve rooms for us?"

The clerk held on firmly. "Excuse me, young lady. The hotel register is strictly confidential." When she let go, he skimmed the pages with his finger. "I have no record of Professor Crockett making reservations for anyone. Perhaps you are mistaken about the time and place you were to meet him."

Katie shook her head. "Not hardly."

"I don't get it." Sam ran his hand through his short blond hair. "Why would Dad tell us to meet him here and then not show up? Something must be wrong."

"That is very puzzling." The clerk snapped the book shut. "But I am sure your father would not want you to stay here under these circumstances. I suggest the three of you consider returning home until the professor contacts you. The airport has flights leaving daily."

"Maybe we shouldn't talk about this right now." Shala glanced around the hotel lobby. There were two men standing near the front door who seemed to be hanging on every word they said. He turned to the clerk and handed him a credit card. "We want two rooms, please."

The man hesitated. "Are you sure this is wise? After all, you have no idea when, or even if, Professor Crockett will return."

"He said we wanted two rooms." Katie

folded her arms. "Your sign outside says you have vacancies. Is there a problem?"

The man swallowed. "How long will you be staying?"

Shala gave the others a warning look. "We're not sure right now. We'll let you know later."

The clerk grudgingly produced two keys. "You are on the second floor at the end of the hall."

"Come on, guys." Shala pretended to yawn and took the keys. "I'm really beat. It's been a long day."

They picked up their luggage and followed Shala to the stairs. At the top of the landing Katie stopped and peeked over her shoulder. The two men who had been waiting by the door had moved to the desk and were talking in whispers to the clerk.

Katie pretended to have trouble with the wheels on her luggage. She knelt and watched the men through the railing. When they turned to leave, one of the men looked up the stairs.

Katie drew a sharp breath. It was the thief from the airport.

CHAPTER 5

"I'm not sure what's going on here, but it looks like Katie is right. Dad's in some kind of trouble." Sam spoke without looking up. He was hunched over a table with a screwdriver in one hand and a bundle of small multicolored wires in the other.

"Great deduction, Sherlock." Katie paced the floor beside the bed. "In case you missed it, we're in trouble too. That clerk downstairs did everything he could to convince us to go home, and the man who stole my bag from the airport is still following us."

She stopped and stared at her brother. "What are you doing? We don't have time right now for you to play junior inventor. We have to figure out what's going on here."

Sam kept working. "I almost have this put together. It's a simple locator. You never know when something like this might come in handy. And besides, working helps me think."

Shala was sitting on one of the hard wooden chairs. He walked over. "It looks a lot like a doorbell. What does it do?"

"You had to ask." Katie plopped on the bed. "Now we'll be here all day."

Sam ignored her. "Actually, it did start out as a doorbell." He popped a battery into the back of one of the pieces and handed it to Shala. "Here, you take the transmitter and go into Katie's room and hide."

"Is anybody listening to me? We don't have time for this." Katie tapped her fingernails impatiently on the headboard.

"It won't take long." Sam waited a few minutes after Shala had gone through the connecting door. Then he pushed a black button on the piece he was holding. They could hear a loud buzzing noise like a ringing doorbell.

Sam picked up the device and stood in the doorway between the two rooms. He opened it and pushed the button again. This time it rang even more loudly. "No contest," Sam called. "You're under the bed."

Shala crawled out. "That thing is great! It's small enough so that you could put it any-where—in your wallet, on your dog, or even on an unsuspecting person."

"That's the idea. It's still got a few bugs, though. I'm trying to increase the range of the transmitter and also put in an optional detec-tor. See this light? Hopefully, when I'm fin-ished you'll have the choice of either hearing the buzzer or seeing a small red flash when it picks up the signal."

"Are we through playing yet?" Katie was standing in the doorway. "Because if we are, I suggest we do something useful, like go look for Dad."

Shala handed the transmitter to Sam. "The main thing is not to panic. If we're going to help Uncle William, we have to go over this whole thing logically, starting from the beginning. How did he wind up down here anyway?"

Katie sat on the edge of the bed. "About six months ago Dad was asked to come to New Mexico to take a look at some ancient ruins that were recently discovered in the wilderness. El Debajo is considered a fantastic find. The only problem is, it has to be handled carefully because of local Native American beliefs. The group sponsoring him knows that Dad has dealt with these sensitive types of situations before, and that's why they hired him."

"How many people are on your father's team?" Shala asked.

"The advance team is usually five archaeologists, including Dad. Normally he picks his own people, but this time there was a hitch. The government got involved and insisted that he work with a couple of their experts. So right now there are only three of them. More will come down if Dad thinks the site is worth it." Katie frowned. "Dad told me that the government was afraid to let too many people in the ruins at once. This area has had a rash of kidnappings lately. It's so close to the border, it's easy for the bad guys to run to Mexico and hide from the authorities."

Sam put his invention on the table. "You think Dad's been kidnapped?"

"At this point we can't be sure of anything." Shala rubbed his temples, trying to concentrate. "The odds are against it. According to the registration clerk, Uncle William has been gone for several days. That's long enough for a ransom note to turn up if somebody was holding him for money. No, there has to be another reason."

Katie started pacing again. "If he hasn't been kidnapped, then where is he?"

There was a soft tap on the door.

"Who's there?" Shala called.

No one answered, but the knob turned and Pepe slid inside the room, quickly closing the door behind him.

"How'd you do that?" Sam asked. "We had that door locked."

"I have many talents." Pepe smiled pleasantly. "My cousin Pancho taught me everything about locks. At times it can be very useful."

"I bet. Did you find out anything about our father?" Katie asked.

"*Sí*. I have information in which you will be interested." Pepe kept his voice low. "Your father and his companions have been working at the Debajo ruins for several months. They often came into San Marcos for supplies. Professor Crockett was last seen here almost three weeks ago. But he and his friends have not been in town since."

"Where are they?" Sam demanded.

"I have put myself in much danger coming here." Pepe held out his hand, palm upward.

Sam gave an exasperated sigh and handed Pepe another dollar. "No more fooling around. Where did they go?"

"No one knows for sure, *señor*. But they are not here. That I can guarantee."

"That's it? That's all you know? Give me my money back, you little bandit. We already figured out that he wasn't here."

Pepe quickly stuffed the bill in his pocket. "There is more. Strangers from across the border have been asking questions about the three of you around the *barrios.* They paid my cousin Felipe a lot of money to keep an eye on you and report everything you do back to them."

Sam's eyes narrowed. "Well, you can tell your cousin—"

"My cousin has to make a living too, *señor*," Pepe interrupted. "He has a wife and two little ones. But do not worry. We have an understanding. He will only report those things we wish him to."

"Why are these people so interested in us?" Shala asked. "And what does it have to do with my uncle's disappearance?"

"These are very bad men, *señor*. It is possible they work for the Cartel, a powerful drug mafia located in Central America. The talk is that they are searching for something valuable which they believe you have." The look on Pepe's face turned grim. "And I am worried they will stop at nothing to get their hands on it."

CHAPTER 6

"Hurry up, Katie!" Sam pounded on her door. "We're supposed to meet Pepe at the market at eight, remember?"

"I'm ready." Katie made sure her papers were safe in the small leather bag she wore around her neck. She opened the door and spoke in a loud voice in case the clerk was listening. "Boy, I can't wait to go shopping. I hear there are tons of great bargains in San Marcos."

Sam winked at her. "Let's go. Shala's already outside holding the taxi."

Katie followed him downstairs to the street

and slid into the backseat of a dilapidated station wagon that had been painted bright yellow.

Shala had already given the driver instructions, and the man whisked them across town to the Plaza Bolivar, a market where New Mexican artisans had their various wares on display in long rows of houses, booths, and tents.

After Sam had paid the driver, they got out and walked to one of the booths. The owner immediately tried to sell them some handmade leather goods.

"What do you need, miss?" He smiled at Katie. "How about a new purse, maybe a money pouch. Just look at the fine craftsmanship. There is none better anywhere."

Katie picked up the *carriel.* "Hey. This is a lot like the little bag Dad sent me to keep my papers in. I wonder if he got it from here?"

"No sale today, Uncle Carlos." Pepe appeared behind them. "These tourists are with me." He motioned for them to follow him.

Katie set the pouch on the counter. "Sorry. Maybe later."

Pepe led them through a maze of chili peppers, handmade baskets, and silver jewelry to a small, dark adobe house that looked as if it had been built centuries earlier. Tiles were missing from the roof and the plaster was peeling off the outside walls. He lifted a brightly colored rug that hung from the doorway and held it up so that they could enter.

The room was dark. A single candle was placed on a small round table in the center of the floor.

"Wait here," Pepe said softly. "I will find out if La Bruja can see you."

"La Bruja?" Sam whispered. "Doesn't that mean—"

"The Witch." Shala nodded. "Why would Pepe bring us here?"

A curtain parted and an elderly woman whose face was so wrinkled it was hard to see her eyes shuffled into the room. "Sit down, *niños*. My great-grandson tells me that you are needy. I will give you a reading."

Katie frowned. "I don't think you understand, ma'am. Pepe told us to come here because we need information about our dad. We really don't have time for anything else."

"Sit," the old woman commanded. She closed her eyes and began swaying back and forth. In moments, a strange, high-pitched wail came from her lips. Then she stopped. Her eyes opened and she stared straight at Katie. She pointed a long, bony finger in Katie's face. "You . . . you have the key. But you must be very careful. I have seen danger. Your friends may be your enemies. And your enemies will come for you. I see that you are part of the legend."

"Legend?" Katie frowned. "I don't know what you're talking about."

The woman put her hand down. "Many thousands of years ago, this land was inhabited almost entirely by Indians. The story is told that one of these primitive tribes was supposed to have built a vast underground fortress for protection against invaders. It is said that when these underground people started digging they discovered rivers of gold in caves beneath the desert floor. But because of their superstitious beliefs, they did not touch it. They only used the gold-filled caverns as burial places to honor their dead. It is also said that these hidden tombs are somewhere near the ruins of El Debajo." The old woman smiled. "Now, tell me how you are connected to the legend."

Katie shook her head. "I'm afraid I don't know. I've never heard it until just now."

La Bruja clapped her hands. "That is all I can see." She stood and walked through the curtain.

Sam rubbed the back of his neck. "Great. I'm sure this will be very helpful. I guess we'd better be going now."

Pepe stood in the doorway, blocking their exit. "My grandmother is a widow with no one to support her. The usual fee for a reading is five American dollars."

Sam sighed and dug into his wallet. "You and your relatives are going to break me."

Katie held up her hand. "This one's on me, Sam. I haven't figured out how we can use it yet, but I think La Bruja may have given us more of a clue than we realize."

CHAPTER 7

It was still early morning, and the market was beginning to fill with people. The sellers noisily called out their wares, and the customers haggled over prices. Three teenagers and a small boy huddled near some large handmade baskets.

"Can you arrange for us to get out of the city without anyone knowing about it?" Shala asked Pepe quietly. "We want to go to the ruins and check things out. If we're lucky, Uncle William could be there, or at least maybe we'll find the other members of his archaeology team."

"There might be a way." Pepe looked thoughtful. "Go back to the hotel and pack your things. Do not go out. Tomorrow morning tell everyone you are taking the bus to the village of El Banco to go sightseeing."

"He just told you, we want to leave without anyone knowing," Katie whispered.

"In San Marcos this is impossible. The next best thing is to try and throw the men who follow you off your trail." Pepe glanced around. "My brother-in-law drives the El Banco bus. Leave everything to me."

"Wait a minute." Sam made a face. "How much is this going to cost us?"

"Only a small fee. Since we are friends, I will give you a good rate. Trust me."

"Oh, I trust you, all right. I trust you to send me back home with an empty wallet."

"Oh no, *señor.*" Pepe winked. "Before you leave New Mexico, I will have your wallet too." He patted Sam on the back. "Now, if you will excuse me, I have many important details to take care of on your behalf. Do not linger too long at the market. It might not be wise."

They watched him disappear into the crowd.

"Where do we go from here?" Katie asked.

"Back to the hotel. Pepe told us to go pack and wait," Sam reminded her.

Katie shrugged. "Pepe is a cute kid and everything, but I don't remember anyone putting him in charge. It's our father who's missing. Don't tell me you want to waste the rest of the day lying around the hotel when we could be out looking for him?"

"I want to find Dad just as much as you do. I just think it would be smarter to play it safe. If we start acting suspicious now, we'll blow everything. And since I'm the oldest—"

"Excuse me. Ten minutes does not make you wise and all-knowing. I think the smartest thing to do is—"

"Time out." Shala stepped between them. "We'll compromise. The odds are whoever is behind all this has their people watching us right now. Since we are tourists, we'll act like it—and while we're at it we'll keep our eyes open for clues. Who knows, maybe something

will turn up. If it doesn't, we go back to the hotel and pack. Agreed?"

Katie nodded grudgingly. Sam turned to study the people coming and going in the market. "I guess since we're already here, the market is as good a place as any to start."

Chapter 8

"So you're Pepe's uncle Carlos?" Katie pretended to be interested in one of the leather shoulder bags on display in his booth. "He seems like such a nice boy."

"Pepe? Oh, he's nice, all right. A little too big for his britches sometimes, but . . . would you like to buy that purse, miss? I can give you a good price. Those happen to be on sale just for today."

"I'm not sure." Katie glanced up and noticed Sam and Shala trying on sombreros at another booth across from her. She stifled a laugh and turned back to the counter. "A purse might be too bulky to carry around." She put it back on the hook and picked up one of the money pouches. "These are pretty. My father bought me one a couple of months ago. He didn't happen to get it here, did he? He's a tall man with brown eyes and a black-and-gray beard? You would have recognized him by his hat. It's one of those 1940s kind, like Indiana Jones wore in the movies."

Carlos thought for a moment and then shook his head. "No. I do not remember anyone like that."

"Well, thanks anyway. Your leather work is beautiful. Maybe I'll come back and buy something before we leave town."

She sighed and turned to walk to the next booth. The last time she had spoken to her father had been a little over three weeks earlier. He had laughed and joked with her. He'd said that this part of New Mexico was almost like a foreign country, instead of part of the United States. He had made no mention of anything being wrong, though. He'd asked if they'd received the presents he had sent them and told her to make sure and keep her ID and traveler's checks in her new money pouch.

She replayed the telephone conversation over and over in her mind, but nothing stood out as a clue.

A booth in the next aisle that sold jewelry caught her attention. She had started for it when someone grabbed her arm. Before she could turn around, a black, smelly sack dropped over her head and was pulled snug around her neck. Two pairs of hands picked her up and carried her off at a run.

Katie tried to fight but couldn't move. She couldn't get any air, and she felt herself starting to lose consciousness.

A door slammed shut and she was dropped on the floor facefirst. Her arms were yanked tightly behind her wrists and secured with a coarse rope.

Somone knelt beside her and spoke in a gruff voice. "I will loosen the cloth from your head. But do not call out or you will regret it."

Katie could feel the heavy material grow slack. She took several deep breaths and choked out, "Who are you? Why are you doing this?"

"Quiet. We will ask the questions. You will answer. Where is the map of El Debajo?"

"What map? I don't know what you're talking about. Let me go." Katie kicked out with her feet.

Someone else in the room laughed. "She has courage, this one. Too bad we may have to get rid of her."

Katie froze. She had heard the slow, even voice before. It was the man from the airport.

"So, you recognize me. Good. Then you know that I mean business. Give us the map and we will let you live."

Katie swallowed. "Where's my father?"

The man kneeling beside her grabbed the back of her hair. "I told you we would ask the questions."

The thief from the airport laughed again. "She doesn't seem to be afraid of us, *amigo*. Why don't you go ahead and tell her what happened to her father? Then perhaps she will change her mind."

The hand on her hair tightened. "Your father made the mistake of double-crossing us. He stole the map and sent it to you. Then he refused to reproduce it for us. Naturally we had no choice but to execute him. If you do not tell us where the map is hidden, you will suffer the same fate."

Katie gasped. She bit her lip and tried to think. She didn't believe these men; they would say anything to scare her. "Do you promise to let me go if I tell you where it is?"

The thief rubbed his hands together. "We are not animals, *señorita.* And of course we have no desire to harm a defenseless girl. But we will have the map—one way or another."

"Then take it. I hid it in my hotel room."

"Do not play games with us. We searched your rooms this morning. There was no map."

"A lot you know. I . . . taped it to the back of the toilet."

The thief snapped his fingers. The grip on her hair loosened, and Katie could hear heavy footsteps leaving the room. "We will check, *señorita.* I hope for your sake you are telling the truth. Just in case, I think it best that you remain here until we return."

The door closed. Katie listened carefully to make sure she was alone. There was no sound other than her own harsh breathing. She rolled over and sat up. The ropes on her wrists cut into her skin.

She tried to shake the black sack off her head, but it refused to budge. Blindly she struggled to her knees and then to her feet.

The hinges on the door squeaked.

"Katie! Are you all right?" Sam rushed to her and pulled the bag off.

She gulped the fresh air. "Fine . . . I'm fine. How did you find me so fast?"

Shala moved to untie her hands. "Sam put the locator in your money pouch while you were in the shower last night. He said you have a tendency to wander off."

The ropes loosened. Katie pulled free and rubbed her wrists. "I guess I should be mad. But for once, I'm glad he acted like a *big* brother. Where are we?"

"In a little house near the market. Who were those thugs?" Sam asked. "We almost ran into them outside. They seemed to be in an awful hurry."

"I'll tell you about it later." Katie went to the door and peeked outside. "Right now we'd better get out of here. Because when they come back, I guarantee—they won't be happy."

CHAPTER 9

"It isn't that I do not believe you, Miss Crockett." The police sergeant walked around his desk. "It is only that you do not have any proof to back up your claims."

"Proof?" Katie's voice rose slightly. "A man threatened to kill me. I have rope burns on both my wrists, not to mention the fact that these people say they've already murdered my father—and you want proof?"

"Please calm yourself." The sergeant reached for a file on his desk. "Look, according to your report, you did not actually see the faces of the men you say kidnapped you at the market. Yet you ask me to send my men out to arrest them. Even if we find someone who fits the description you give of the so-called thief at the airport, we would not be able to hold him on such flimsy evidence."

"What about our rooms?" Sam asked. "You saw them. Those guys trashed our stuff."

The sergeant scratched his head. "It is a sad fact that this kind of thing is a common occurrence in San Marcos. If we only had more officers . . ."

Shala stood. "I think we've taken up enough of the sergeant's time. He obviously has bigger things to worry about. In the morning we'll do like we planned and go see the sights at El Banco. And if we don't hear from Uncle William by the time we get back to San Marcos, we will have no choice but to fly home and wait until he contacts us. Let's go."

"But . . . ," Katie protested.

"Shala's right, Katie." Sam took her elbow and said in a low voice, "Remember what La Bruja said about your friends being your enemies?"

Katie turned to the officer. "It's been a long day. We're going to our hotel now. If anything turns up, you know where to find us."

The sergeant walked them to the door. "Enjoy your trip to El Banco. It is a colorful village, and I'm sure it will make you forget your troubles. Hopefully when you return I will have some news for you about your father."

Outside the police station Katie shuffled despondently to the curb to look for a taxi.

Shala stopped her. "Don't look so down. Those crooks were lying about Uncle William. They'd say anything to get you to talk. We have to use the information they gave you to try and find him, that's all. If we put our heads together I bet we can figure out where this mysterious map is hiding."

"I told you," Katie sighed. "Dad didn't send me a map. He sent Sam a poncho, which is now hanging from the ceiling fan in his bedroom, and he sent me a leather money pouch to keep my papers in."

"Did you check the pouch? Maybe he hid the map in the lining or one of the pockets."

Katie nodded. "I looked. There's no lining

and only one pocket. The map couldn't be hidden in it. There's no place to conceal it."

Shala rubbed his forehead. After a few moments his eyes narrowed. "Can I see the pouch?"

"Sure. I have it right here." She slid the chain over her head and handed it to him. "But I'm telling you, there's no map in it."

Shala unzipped the pouch and looked inside. Then he ran his fingers over the strange design on the cover.

"Uncle William did send you a map, Katie. You've had it with you all the time."

Katie looked at Shala. Suddenly she saw what he meant.

"Of course," she whispered. "I should have known it wouldn't be inside the pouch." She stood next to him and studied the detailed configuration on the front. "The map is on the outside. Dad had it carved into the leather."

Chapter 10

"They call this a road? It feels more like a cattle trail." Sam bounced in his seat and came down hard.

"We're taking a shortcut." Katie held on to the back of the seat in front of her. "You heard Pepe's brother-in-law. He said this way was better for tourists because it's more scenic."

"Scenic?" Sam glanced out the window. "The only things out there for the last twenty miles have been cactus, sand, and flies."

"Not exactly." Shala made a quick scan of the other passengers on the bus. No one was paying any attention, and they all appeared to be local people. He motioned to the window. "Take another look."

Sam squinted. Ahead and to the right of the bus were some chalk-colored hills that seemed out of place in the flat desert landscape.

The bus slowed down and then stopped. Pepe's brother-in-law put the emergency brake on and opened the doors. He jumped out and raised the hood.

"This is it, guys." Shala stood up. "Let's go see if we can *help* the driver." Katie and Sam nodded and followed him down the aisle.

Outside, Pepe's brother-in-law didn't say a word. He just pointed at the chalk hills, closed the hood, and got back into his bus. The engine started, and black smoke billowed from the exhaust as it pulled away.

"I'm not so sure about this." Sam watched the bus until it was out of sight. "How do we know we're not being set up?"

A donkey brayed.

Shala's head went up. "Sounds like our ride is waiting." He walked across the sand and disappeared behind the first hill. "Over here," he called.

Katie and Sam sprinted up the hill. On the other side, Pepe was sitting by a small campfire roasting a hot dog on the end of a greasewood stick. Four donkeys were hobbled nearby.

"*Buenos dias,* good morning, my friends. Would you care for a snack? I suggest you eat and drink. It may be the last chance you get for some time."

"No thanks," Sam said. "We had a good breakfast in San Marcos and we're kind of in a hurry."

Pepe stuffed the hot dog into his mouth and kicked sand on the fire. "See how I try to please?"

They watched as he quickly unhobbled the donkeys. "You would not believe what a good price I was able to get for you on these fine burros."

"I can just imagine." Sam took the reins of the first one and hopped on. "When we get back to San Marcos you can send me your bill."

"There is no need. Because I knew you would want to pay me as soon as possible, I brought the bill with me. If you wish to pay me now, you may."

"I don't wish," Sam growled. "Which way to the ruins?"

"Oh, you would like me to also be your guide. I would be glad to do that—"

Shala interrupted, "For a small fee, of course."

Pepe crawled onto his donkey and nudged it out in front of the others. "Of course."

Katie shook her head. "That boy will be a millionaire by the time he's a teenager."

"Yeah," Sam muttered. "And most of it will be *my* money."

A whirlwind kicked up dust and carried it across the trail. Pepe stopped until it passed, and then continued at a trot. He rode without looking back for almost an hour.

"This is worse than the bus," Sam complained. "My legs hurt and my insides feel like they're about to come out my ears. How much longer?"

Pepe pulled his donkey to a halt and slid

off. "I think this is a good place to stop." He tied the reins to a mesquite limb and started to remove the blanket from the burro's back. "There is sand grass here. Enough to keep the burros happy until you return."

Katie stepped to the ground. "What do you mean, until *we* return? Aren't you coming with us?"

"Sorry. A few hundred yards ahead there is a long wooden bridge that the donkeys will be afraid to cross. Since I am responsible for their well-being I must stay with them. But do not worry. After you cross the bridge, the ruins will not be far away."

Pepe knelt and, using a stick, drew a map in the sand. "I have not been to the site myself, but these are reliable directions, according to my uncle Francisco."

"How many times has he been to the site?" Shala asked.

"He has not been there either. But he has heard talk."

"Great." Sam shook his legs out. "So what you're telling us is that you're sending us on a wild-goose chase. All I can say is you'd better be here when we get back.''

"I would never leave my friends in such a place as this.'' Pepe took the reins from Sam. "Especially friends who owe me money.''

CHAPTER 11

"This must be the bridge Pepe was talking about." Shala frowned. "I can see why the donkeys wouldn't want any part of it." He looked across the canyon that the bridge crossed. It was as wide as it was deep. The bridge over it was made of planks held together by old rope.

"I'm not sure I want any part of it either." Sam shook the rope railing. One of the planks fell out, plummeting until it fell out of sight far below. "Maybe we should look for another way around. There has to be one. Dad wouldn't have come this way."

"Pepe said this way was the fastest." Katie shoved Sam in front of her. "You go first."

"Why should I?"

Katie folded her arms. "Because you're the oldest, remember?"

"True." Sam stepped up to the bridge and stopped. "But then, I'm also the best-looking and the smartest and—"

"Oh, please." Katie pushed past him and walked onto the bridge. "It seems sturdy enough. Just be careful—and whatever you do, don't let go of the rope." She took a few more steps and looked back. "What are you guys waiting for?"

Shala put his finger to his lips and listened. "Did you hear that?"

The hum of an engine was getting closer. In the distance they could see a cloud of dust moving toward them.

"Hurry! Somebody's coming." Katie bolted across the bridge, taking giant steps.

Shala was more cautious. He worked his way over the shaky boards with Sam following close behind.

The boys were halfway across when two

motorcycles roared up behind them. It was the thief from the airport and a tall, heavyset man.

"You lied to us, *senorita*!" the thief yelled. "That was not a very smart thing to do." He began to roll his motorcycle onto the bridge. "Especially since now you will have to give us the map anyway."

Katie stepped off the bridge on the far side and felt in her pocket for the army knife she carried with her. She unfolded the sharpest blade and began sawing on the rope.

"What are you doing?" Sam shouted.

Shala's eyes narrowed. "I think she means it. Hang on to the rope—and hurry."

The boys started running. They leaped onto solid ground as the first strand of the rope railing snapped.

There was a loud pop, and the bridge flopped up and down in heaving waves. One side dropped, and several planks fell to the canyon floor.

The thief moved back. "It won't do you any good to destroy the bridge. We know another way into the ruins. Eventually you will have to give us the map."

Katie ignored him and started sawing on the other railing.

The thief burst out with a stream of Spanish words and shook his fist at them. The two men turned their motorcycles around, started the engines, and drove away.

"Are you crazy?" Sam sprang to his feet and grabbed Katie's knife. "You could have killed us."

"But I didn't, did I? I saved us."

"For now." Shala brushed the dirt off his jeans. "That was pretty scary."

"Sorry. It just seemed like there weren't a lot of choices. Those two play rough. Believe me, I know how they operate firsthand."

Shala pointed south. "According to Pepe's drawing, we should head this way." He started walking. "The ruins are supposed to be at the mouth of the next canyon. Let's go."

Katie turned to ask Sam for her knife. Her mouth fell open. "Did you see that?"

"See what?" Shala asked.

"The old Indian. He was standing right over there, plain as day. Then he just disappeared."

"I knew we should have brought water," Sam said. "She's hallucinating."

"I am not. I saw him. He was right there."

"Even if someone was there, we don't have time to investigate." Shala kept walking. "If we're going to find any answers in the ruins we'd better get there first."

CHAPTER 12

"I can see why your dad wanted to come here. This is great." Shala pointed above them. "Look at that. It's like they built an apartment complex right into the side of the canyon."

"Dad called them cliff dwellers." Sam ran his hand over a crumbling dirt wall. "I wonder how old all this is."

Katie poked her head out of one of the tents they had discovered nearby. "I double-checked. All Dad's stuff is gone. There's no sign of his two assistants either. Somebody has already been here and taken everything."

Shala ran his hand through his hair. "Where could Uncle William be?" He sat down on a rock. "Let's have another look at the map. Maybe we'll see something we missed before."

Katie took the purse out. "We've been over it a million times." She walked to the crumbling wall. "The pattern shows the ruins, a stream, a bunch of dots, and something that looks like a big hole near the top of the canyon face, with trails leading everywhere. The only problem is, we can't see any hole from down here, and we didn't find any trails."

A shower of dirt and rocks fell from above them. Katie looked up and saw a man standing near the top of the canyon.

"It's him! It's the old Indian I saw before."

"I think he wants us to follow him." Sam scratched his head. "But how did he get up there? There's no ladder."

"He climbed." Shala moved to the canyon face and pointed at some small indentations that went all the way up. "There are your dots, Katie. They're footholds."

The roar of engines broke the stillness of the desert.

Sam put his foot into one of the small crevices. "If we're going to climb it, I think we'd better hustle."

A rope dropped down to them.

"All right." Sam grabbed it and yanked. It was tied solid. He began pulling himself up. A few yards from the top, a hand reached out and helped him inside a narrow opening in the canyon wall.

The Indian knelt and waited for Shala. The engines were getting closer. Katie started to climb the rope and then changed her mind.

She yelled up, "I'll never make it in time. Don't worry about me. I know a good hiding place." She darted to the nearest tent.

Shala swung into the same opening as Sam, and the rope snaked back up the wall and out of sight.

The two motorcycles came to a stop a few feet from the tent. Katie closed her eyes and hoped the men would be fooled into thinking she and the boys had already left.

She could hear them talking and walking around outside. The thief sounded angry.

The tent flap was thrown back, and the men stomped inside. Katie held her breath. The thief was yelling at the other man in Spanish. In a fit of temper, he slammed the toe of his boot into the side of the trunk Katie was hiding in.

Suddenly the lid jerked open. The thief looked down at Katie, grinning. He waved his gun. "I might have never found you, but your father's trunk should have sounded hollow, empty, when I kicked it. Too bad for you, *señorita*. Where are your companions?"

Katie swallowed. "They heard you coming and went for help."

"And left you all alone? Somehow I doubt that. No matter. Give us the map and you can all be on your way home."

"I don't believe you. You already said you killed my father."

The heavyset man lifted her out of the trunk and held her a few feet off the ground. "And we will kill you too, little girl—if you don't give us the map."

"Yoo-hoo! We're over here!" A barrage of small rocks hit the front of the tent.

Katie went limp. It was Sam. She had hoped the boys would stay hidden.

The thief motioned to the door. "Go take care of that, Zamora. I'll keep an eye on her."

The big man set Katie down and walked out of the tent. Instantly she heard a loud thud and the sound of someone falling.

The thief grabbed Katie's arm. He held her in front of him and forced her through the tent flap.

Outside there was no sign of anyone.

"Zamora? Where are you?" the thief called out.

"It's the ghosts of the Indians who used to live here." Katie tried to pull away. "They got him."

"Let the girl go, Señor Vasquez. You are surrounded."

Katie's eyes widened. She didn't see anyone, but she recognized the voice of the police sergeant from San Marcos.

"Show yourself," Vasquez called. "Perhaps we can make a trade. The map for the girl."

"Look up there." Katie pointed to the ledge. The old Indian was standing there, right in front of the hidden opening, but from below, it looked as if he were floating in air. "I told you—it's a ghost!"

Vasquez stared. He blinked and then aimed his gun at the Indian. Katie elbowed him in the stomach as hard as she could. The gun fell from his hand.

The police sergeant rushed from behind a boulder and kicked the weapon away. He held his gun on the thief. "Don't move."

Sam scrambled out from behind a creosote bush. "Katie, are you all right?"

"I'm fine." She watched the sergeant tie up the thief. "But how—"

"You have me to thank, *señorita*." Pepe stepped around the tent. "I told my uncle Francisco that you were going to the ruins. It was he who suggested following you just in case you ran into trouble. And when I heard the sound of motorcycles, I was sure you would need my help also."

"The police sergeant is your uncle?" Katie demanded. "Why didn't you tell us?"

"You did not ask," Pepe said, shrugging.

The sergeant winked at her as he marched his second captive to a flat rock and ordered him to sit.

"Hey, everybody," Shala yelled down from the opening. "Look who I found."

Katie covered her eyes and squinted up. Her breath caught in her throat.

The bandaged face of her father peered down at her.

Chapter 13

Katie brought her father a second cup of coffee from the machine in the police station's lobby. He gave her a warm smile and then went on with his story.

"I was suspicious of Vasquez and Zamora right from the start. They didn't seem to know much about archaeology, and yet they claimed to be the advance team sent down by the government to help me on the El Debajo dig. It was Isaac here who told me what they were up to."

The tall Indian stood nearby with his arms

folded. He nodded at the professor and talked to him in sign language.

"You see, Isaac is a descendant of the original cliff dwellers. Unfortunately, he can't speak, but that didn't stop him from being very concerned about the way the digging at the ruins would be handled. When he overheard those two imposters talking about exploiting the burial caves and stealing the artifacts, Isaac gave me his great-grandfather's map for safekeeping."

"And then you carved a copy of it on my money pouch and sent it to me so the crooks wouldn't get it." Katie held the pouch out for the sergeant to see.

"Right. Only at the time, I had no idea how desperate those two really were. They believed the old stories about the rivers of gold." The professor touched the bandages on his head. "One night they ambushed me, tied me up, and left me in a ditch. If it hadn't been for Isaac, I might not have made it. He carried me to the hidden burial tunnels and took care of my wounds. I was delirious for several days."

"What about the legend?" Sam asked. "Are

there really underground caverns of gold near the ruins?''

"It's doubtful. But Isaac says there are miles of hand-dug tunnels. And the cliff dwellers were known to bury certain items they considered valuable with their dead. If we can find some of them it could help us understand their culture better. When I feel a little stronger, we'll take Katie's map and go exploring.''

"I am glad to see that you are recovering, Professor.'' The sergeant put down his pen and notepad. "Your children and nephew were quite worried about you.''

"I know. I just wish I had found out about Vasquez and Zamora in time to warn them. If I had been paying better attention, maybe I could have prevented all this from happening.''

"Oh, they were never in any real danger, *señor*,'' Pepe said pleasantly. "I was taking very good care of them.''

"He sure was,'' Sam said sarcastically. "For a price.''

Pepe looked hurt. "Are you saying that you

are dissatisfied with my work? Did I not do everything you asked?"

"And then some." Shala patted Pepe on the shoulder. "Bringing your uncle to the ruins was beyond the call of duty."

"It sure was," Katie assured him. "Without you, those two thieves might have gotten away with their rotten plan. Isn't that right, Sam?"

"Okay. I guess we do owe him. How much is it going to cost me this time?" Sam reached into his back pocket. "My wallet. It's gone!"

"Looking for this?" Pepe grinned and dangled the wallet in front of him. "My friend, you already paid for the donkeys and also gave your trustworthy guide a very unselfish tip."

"How nice of me." Sam grabbed the wallet. "Do I have anything left?"

"Enough. Of course I would be glad to help you spend the rest. It so happens, I have an aunt who makes the finest enchiladas and *menudo* in all New Mexico." Pepe moved to the door. "I will take you there. It will cost you practically nothing."

"Enchiladas sound great." Katie winked at her dad and Shala. "I am so lucky to have such a wise and generous *older* brother."

Professor Crockett scratched his head. "Am I missing something here?"

Sam looked into his wallet and sighed. "No, Dad—it looks like I'm the one who's missing something."

GARY PAULSEN
ADVENTURE GUIDE

THE CLIFF DWELLERS

In the southwestern United States and northern Mexico, evidence still stands of ancient peoples who built their villages high in the faces of sheer canyon walls. These ancient Indians are now called the Anasazi, which means "the ancient ones."

Almost every facet of the cliff dwellers' lives was conducted high above the canyon floor. Families slept and stored their possessions in small, cell-like rooms, which opened onto a common courtyard. Here they held religious ceremonies, worked, cooked, ate, and played. The cliff dwellers grew crops, hunted, and searched for roots and berries. Water was a problem; they had to carry it from springs below their homes and store it in jars.

Hundreds of people could live in the cliff dwellings, which were easy to defend from outside attack. Shouts of warning that enemies were entering the canyon echoed loudly off the rock walls. And when the ladders and ropes to the cliff dwellings' en-

trances were lifted, the only way to reach them was by handholds and footholds carved into the sides of the sandstone walls.

The Anasazi felt safe in their cliff fortresses, but drought and new enemies eventually drove them from their caves, and they moved south and east. Their descendants can be found among the present-day Pueblo Indians.

Don't miss all the exciting action!

**Read the other action-packed books in
Gary Paulsen's
WORLD OF ADVENTURE!**

The Legend of Red Horse Cavern

Will Little Bear Tucker and his friend Sarah Thompson have heard the eerie Apache legend many times. Will's grandfather especially loves to tell them about Red Horse—an Indian brave who betrayed his people, was beheaded, and now haunts the Sacramento Mountain range, searching for his head. To Will and Sarah it's just a story—until they decide to explore a new-found mountain cave, a cave filled with danger-ous treasures.

Deep underground, Will and Sarah uncover an old chest stuffed with a million dollars. But now armed bandits are after them. When they find a gold Apache statue hidden in a skull, it seems Red Horse is hunting them, too. Then they lose their way, and each step they take in the damp, dark cavern could be their last.

Rodomonte's Revenge

Friends Brett Wilder and Tom Houston are video game whizzes. So when a new virtual re-ality arcade called Rodomonte's Revenge opens near their home, they make sure they're its first customers. The game is awesome. There are flaming fire rivers to jump, beastly buzz-bugs to fight, and ugly tunnel spiders to escape. If they're good enough they'll face Rodomonte, an evil giant waiting to do battle within his hidden castle.

But soon after they play the game, strange things start happening to Brett and Tom. The computer is taking over their minds. Now everything that happens in the game is happening in real life. A buzz-bug could gnaw off their ears. Rodomonte could smash them to bits. Brett and Tom have no choice but to play Rodomonte's Revenge again. This time they'll be playing for their lives.

Escape from Fire Mountain

". . . please, anybody . . . fire . . . need help."

That's the urgent cry thirteen-year-old Nikki Roberts hears over the CB radio the weekend she's left alone in her family's hunting lodge. The message also says that the sender is trapped near a bend in the river. Nikki knows it's dangerous, but she has to try to help. She paddles her canoe downriver, coming closer to the thick black smoke of the forest fire with each stroke. When she reaches the bend, Nikki climbs onshore. There, covered with soot and huddled on a rock ledge, sit two small children.

Nikki struggles to get the children to safety. Flames roar around them. Trees splinter to the ground. But as Nikki tries to escape the fire, she doesn't know that two poachers are also hot on her trail. They fear that she and the children have seen too much of their illegal operation—and they'll do anything to keep the kids from making it back to the lodge alive.

The Rock Jockeys

Devil's Wall.

Rick Williams and his friends J.D. and Spud—the Rock Jockeys—are attempting to become the first and youngest climbers to ascend the north face of their area's most treacherous mountain. They're also out to discover if a B-17 bomber rumored to have crashed into the mountain years ago is really there.

As the Rock Jockeys explore Devil's Wall, they stumble upon the plane's battered shell. Inside, they find items that seem to have belonged to the crew, including a diary written by the navigator. Spud later falls into a deep hole and finds something even more frightening: a human skull and bones. To find out where they might have come from, the boys read the navigator's story in the diary. It reveals a gruesome secret that heightens the dangers the mountain might hold for the Rock Jockeys.

Hook 'Em, Snotty!

Bobbie Walker loves working on her grandfather's ranch. She hates the fact that her cousin Alex is coming up from Los Angeles to visit and will probably ruin her summer. Alex can barely ride a horse and doesn't know the first thing about roping. There is no way Alex can survive a ride into the flats to round up wild cattle. But Bobbie is going to have to let her tag along anyway.

Out in the flats the weather turns bad. Even worse, Bobbie knows that she'll have to watch out for the Bledsoe boys, two mischievous brothers who are usually up to no good. When the boys rustle the girls' cattle, Bobbie and Alex team up to teach the Bledsoes a lesson. But with the wild bull Diablo on the loose, the fun and games may soon turn deadly serious.

Danger on Midnight River

Daniel Martin doesn't want to go to Camp Eagle Nest. He wants to spend the summer as he always does: with his uncle Smitty in the Rocky Mountains. Daniel is a slow learner, but most other kids call him retarded. Daniel knows that at camp, things are only going to get worse. His nightmare comes true when he and three bullies must ride the camp van together.

On the trip to camp, Daniel is the butt of the bullies' jokes. He ignores them and concentrates on the roads outside. He thinks they may be lost. As the van crosses a wooden bridge, the planks suddenly give way. The van plunges into the raging river below. Daniel struggles to shore, but the driver and the other boys are nowhere to be found. It's freezing, and night is setting in. Daniel faces a difficult decision. He could save himself . . . or risk everything to try to rescue the others, too.

The Gorgon Slayer

Eleven-year-old Warren Trumbull has a strange job. He works for Prince Charming's Damsel in Distress Rescue Agency, saving people from hideous monsters, evil warlocks, and wicked witches. Then one day Warren gets the most dangerous assignment of all: He must exterminate a Gorgon.

Gorgons are horrible creatures. They have green scales, clawed fingers, and snakes for hair. They also have the power to turn people to stone. Warren doesn't want to be a stone statue for the rest of his life. He'll need all his courage and skill—and his secret plan—to become a true Gorgon slayer.

The Gorgon howls as Warren enters the dark basement to do battle. Warren lowers his eyes, raises his sword and shield, and leaps into action. But will his plan work?

Captive!

Roman Sanchez is trying hard to deal with the death of his dad—a SWAT team member gunned down in the line of duty. But Roman's nightmare is just beginning.

When masked gunmen storm into his classroom, Roman and three other boys are taken hostage. They are thrown into the back of a truck and hauled to a run-down mountain cabin, miles from anywhere. They are bound with rope and given no food. With each passing hour the kidnappers' deadly threats become even more real.

Roman knows time is running out. Now he must somehow put his dad's death behind him so that he and the others can launch a last desperate fight for freedom.

The Treasure of El Patrón

Tag Jones and his friend Cowboy spend their days diving in the azure water surrounding Bermuda. It's not just for fun—Tag knows that somewhere in the coral reef there's a sunken ship full of treasure. His father died in a diving accident looking for the ship, and Tag won't give up until he finds it.

Then the ship's manifest of the Spanish galleon *El Patrón* turns up, and Tag can barely contain his excitement. *El Patrón* sank in 1614, carrying "unknown cargo." Tag knows that *this* is the ship his father was looking for. And he's not the least bit scared off by the rumors that *El Patrón* is cursed. But when two tourists want Tag to retrieve some mysterious sunken parcels for them, Tag and Cowboy may be in dangerous water, way over their heads!

Skydive!

Jesse Rodriguez has a pretty exciting job for a thirteen-year-old, working at a small flight and skydiving school near Seattle. Buck Sellman, the owner of the school, lets Jesse help out around the airport and is teaching him all about skydiving. Jesse can't wait until he's sixteen and old enough to make his first jump.

Then Robin Waterford walks in with her father one day to sign up for lessons, and strange things start to happen. Photographs that Robin takes of the airfield mysteriously disappear from her locker. And Robin and Jesse discover that someone at the airfield is involved in an illegal transportation operation. Jesse and Robin soon find themselves in the middle of real danger and are forced to make their first skydives very unexpectedly—using only one parachute!

The Seventh Crystal

Chosen One,
The ancient palace lies in the Valley of Zon. It is imperative that you come immediately. You

are my last hope. Look for the secret path. The stars will lead the way. Take care. The eyes of Mogg are everywhere.

As if school bullies weren't enough of a problem, now Chris Masters has a computer game pushing him around! Ever since The Seventh Crystal arrived anonymously in the mail one day, Chris has been obsessed with it—it's the most challenging game he's ever played. But when the game starts to take over, Chris is forced to face a lean, mean, *medieval* bully.

The Creature of Black Water Lake

Thirteen-year-old Ryan Swanner and his mom just moved to the mountain resort of Black Water Lake. The locals say that beneath the lake's seemingly calm surface, a giant, ancient creature lives. But Ryan's new friend Rita tells him that's just hogwash. She's not afraid to go fishing out on the lake, even though, oddly, the lake seems to be nearly empty of fish. One day Ryan sees a small animal fall from a tree into the lake—and never surface again. Something *is* in the lake. And it's alive. . . .

Time Benders

Superbrain Zack Griffin and hoops fanatic Jeff Brown wouldn't normally hang together. But when both boys win trips to a famous science laboratory, they find out they have one thing in common: a serious case of curiosity. And when they sneak into the lab to check out the time-bending machine again, they end up in Egypt—in 1350 B.C.!

Grizzly

Justin swallowed and pointed the light at the soft dirt. The tracks were plain: two large pads with five long scissorlike claws on each.

A grizzly.

A grizzly bear is terrorizing the sheep ranch that belongs to Justin McCallister's aunt and uncle. First the grizzly takes a swipe at the ranch's guard dog, Old Molly. Then he kills several sheep and injures Justin's collie, Radar. When the grizzly kills Blue, Justin's pet lamb, Justin decides to take matters into his own hands. He sets out to track down the bear himself. But what will Justin do when he comes face to face with the grizzly?

Thunder Valley

Jeremy Parsons and his twin brother, Jason, have been left on their own to run the family business, Thunder Valley Ski Lodge. But ever since Grandpa broke his hip and Grandma went with him to the hospital, strange things have been happening. Things even stranger than the fire in the snowmobile garage . . . Jason and Jeremy had bettter find out who's responsible, because Thunder Valley is going downhill fast.